PRAISE FOR THE MONSTER OPERA

"The Monster Opera is a brilliant and beautiful work, a rising crescendo of action in a haunting tale of love. Many authors strive for that perfect note, yet Stohlman does the unbelievable, turning words on the page into a truly operatic monster which comes alive in the very first scene."

--J.A. Kazimer, author of *Dopesick: A Love Story* and *Shank*

"At one point I found myself pledging my life and allegiance like an old Camelot knight to the life and the legacy of the Opera. If a dragon were to threaten it for some dragon reason, I would've totally put down this pint of whiskey and slain it. Because this Opera must live on! Its safety is more important than my own."

--Rob Geisen, author of *The Aftermath, Etc.*

"In a swell of lyrical prose that drips itself across the borders of music and literature, Nancy Stohlman delivers a self-aware story that sings out from the page like an opera trapped in the belly of an Old World curse. A love affair drunk on magical realism, somehow as ancient as it is avant-garde. "

--Kona Morris, author of *Godless Comics*

"I don't know shit about opera, and many would say less about literature. But I know plenty about these kind of monsters. And I know for damn sure you should be reading Nancy Stohlman."

-- Benjamin Whitmer, author of *Satan Is Real: The Ballad of the Louvin Brothers*

THE MONSTER OPERA

NANCY STOHLMAN

BARTLEBY SNOPES PRESS

The Monster Opera
by Nancy Stohlman

Original Music by Nick Busheff

First Edition, August 2013.

ISBN: 978-1-304-21205-4

Cover design by **Marta Burton**
Cover photo: "Spiral Galaxy" by **George Crumb**
Cover photo by **Nancy Stohlman**
Book design by **Nathaniel Tower**

Some parts of this flash novel have been previously excerpted or published. The author and publisher would like to thank all the journals and editors who published excerpts of this book in its many former incarnations, including: *Spine Road, Lady Jane's Miscellany, Dinosaur Bees* and *Zero Ducats*.

Published by BARTLEBY SNOPES PRESS. For more information about this book or other titles, visit bartlebysnopes.com.

Special thanks to composer Nick Busheff

THE MONSTER OPERA

The Monster Opera

Overture

I hate this story. I hate the Muse. I hate everyone involved in this nightmare and I hate myself. Had anyone tried to warn me when I boarded that plane for Mexico City, I never would have believed them. Now it's a bastard deformity. Not an opera, not a novel. I wish I'd never written the first word. I had no idea what kind of monster I was growing.

The Monster Opera

a flash novel in two acts

Setting

Mexico City

Characters

Ursula Leonard—the writer

Libretto Santiago—tenor

Magdelena Santiago—soprano

Hugo Leonard—the composer

The Traitor—baritone

The Maid

The Muse

ACT ONE

(**Bold** text is sung)

LIBRETTO

If I tell you, you can't keep it.

URSULA

I know.

LIBRETTO

You could be lying. You are a writer, after all.

URSULA

I probably am.

LIBRETTO

I could make you the greatest writer that ever lived. Tell me, do you love me?

URSULA

Maybe...what do you want from me in return?

LIBRETTO

I want your loyalty.

URSULA

But you'll never believe me.

LIBRETTO

What I want doesn't come with words. It comes at a price.

URSULA

And if I agree?

LIBRETTO

Then we are forever linked. Everything I have, including my story, will be yours.

URSULA

And if I don't?

LIBRETTO

Then you should leave this place, leave my bed, leave this house and find yourself another. I'm sure there've been dozens already, offering stories for only a fluttery look. But those were the stories of boys, my dear. You can write their childish tales forever or you can pay the price. I think you'll find it worth the cost.

URSULA

Then I agree.

This is the final moment before the story changes hands, the moment your ego has done you in. You're too infatuated to think straight, you find the prospect of becoming a character romantic and appealing, you want to be immortalized in words, you want to feel that your story is worth taking, Later, when it's too late, you'll forget that you gave it willingly. I warned you.

LIBRETTO

(ARIA)

You must pay the price

The bite was swift and deep in the fleshy part of her shoulder, followed by a warm numbness that made her arm heavy, like a tetanus shot.

The Forbidden Story: Part One

URSULA

The whole family suffered from sad sickness. Even the maid slipped on the somberness with her uniform, and the paper still came day in and day out, though no one had read it in eighteen years. The house smelled of antiques, Grecian fireplaces and carved Spanish doorways and stone monoliths of Poseidon and Athena and the twin sphinxes with lion bodies and Victorian women's faces and the antique carousel horse and the 400-pound chandeliers that distorted the light and scattered it in tiny rainbows. Everything was covered in a layer of age that couldn't be wiped away no matter how often you dusted. Charms guarded every corner and hung from every archway, Jesus and Mary candles on the ancient baby grand piano, gargoyle masks and reflective mirrors and beaded curtains from the Yucatan to filter out the bad spirits. The walls were filled with opera programs and old newspaper clippings behind clouded glass: *Aida, La Boheme, The Magic Flute.*

The staircase was slick, icy even with the space heaters, square slabs of marble geometrically askew.

You could never be warm in the bathrooms, no matter how long you ran the water. The sun never came in the windows except in the nursery. Maybe it was the angle of the building, the way the trees and bougainvillea covered the windows, but it was only in the nursery, with its dark red carpeting, where you could warm for a moment.

In the distance, the two volcanoes: Iztachataltan, the endlessly sleeping woman, Popotechatlan, her lover, in eternal watch. Most days pollution in Mexico City was so thick you couldn't even see them. Yet they were there all the time, nineteen thousand feet of rumbling activity.

When I arrived at the large, lonely mansion of Libretto and Magdelena Santiago, the sad sickness had spanned many decades. I suspected I was the first guest in years. There were no grandbabies, no husbands, wives, no boyfriends, girlfriends, no in-laws. Magdelena, the aging matriarch, must have been stunning once. Smoking had obliterated her soprano voice; her skin was a thin parchment map that had been lifted, tucked, refolded. Once flamboyant and fiery, the daughter of wealthy Spanish doctors, she had married down, an Armenian refugee with a Spanish name. Now she moved through the hallways like a cursed woman, a dramatic white streak through her red hair, wiping dust from picture frames with her fingers.

A spider crawled across the keys of the piano. Magdelena broke the silence.

MAGDELENA

There is a saying in Spain:
A spider in the morning brings sadness
A spider at night brings hope
kill it in the morning kills sadness
kill it in the evening kills hope.
Spiders that bite,
Spiders that crawl,
Spiders in the morning must kill them all!
Spiders that bite must kill them all!
Spiders in the morning that crawl!

MAGDELENA

Spider Song

URSULA

So should we kill it?

MAGDELENA

Oh I just leave them.

~pause~

He always said we would write an opera together.

URSULA

What about?

MAGDELENA

Love. All couples in love want to write about love.

URSULA

You could still write it.

MAGDELENA

It's too late for me to write about love.

~pause~

You have what you came for. If I were you I would get out of here quickly and write it down before it's too late.

Go.

MAGDELENA

The Widow's Lament (ARIA)

Oh, Wicked Past

Prague Times, November 12, 19___

RUSALKA

"Poor, pale Rusalka!" The Water Gnome sings this haunting motif throughout Dvorak's obscure, rarely performed opera, *Rusalka.* Rusalka is willing to bargain potential damnation for this chance at human love, doomed already as she sings her aria "Song to the Moon."

As the cursed water sprite, soprano Magdelena Basco steals the show, withering first at the Prince's castle and then finally as a raif, an undead spirit haunting the forest glen. She layers the lavish, magical set with her ethereal voice and her performance, as we've come to expect from the young soprano, is an inspired combination of fragile and tragic. At an age when many of her peers are still maturing into their voices, Ms. Basco's haunting arias belie a sophistication well beyond her years.

URSULA

I woke in the Santiago mansion to scratch marks across red Egyptian-cotton sheets. My arm ached where I'd been bitten. A hole with a tiny bit of foam oozed from my pillow where it had been pierced. Long maroon streaks striped my arms and legs where The Forbidden Story grew inside of me. My breasts were stretched and sore. Oil glossed my hair, left a marmalade sheen across my cheeks. The story was growing stronger; it was swelling, transforming. I ate cottage cheese, spinach, eggs. I ate raw liver.

HUGO (voice-over)

My Dearest Ursula,

I can't tell you how happy I was to receive your letter—not hearing from you these long months has, of course, planted the most horrific images in my head. I was thrilled to hear of your encounter with such a big, important family—how fortunate to be passing your time in someone's home, rather than alone in some dirty hotel as I feared. And so coincidental that this should be the home of opera singers! Tell me their names, tell me everything about them—perhaps I know them from my younger days?

I didn't want to let you go, but you were right—it was time to find us another story. But in exchange for letting you go I want you to tell me everything, don't leave out a single detail. Even if you think it's trivial I want you to hide nothing. The mood you set when you describe the sadness of the house is perfect for our next creation. I've begun composing The Overture. I call it The Sad Sickness. I hope you like it.

Your adoring husband,
Hugo

Sad Sickness musical solo

(insert sheet music)

The Forbidden Story: Part Two

URSULA

Armenia—land of fables and superstitions, land of Van, the flying winged dragon of myth, land of enchanted forests and mythical creatures...neighbor to Romania, Transylvania. Armenia. The first country ever to convert to Christianity. And why? Why was the emperor of Armenia so eager to convert? Perhaps he already knew something that others did not.

On that horrible night the main church in the town of Van was full—250 of the town's intellectuals rounded up and crammed inside.

But the 250 gathered in the church had something else in common.

Libretto was only five years old the day he watched his father rounded up with the others. Before his father had been taken away he had called the boy to him: What do you want to be more than anything in the world, son?

The world's greatest tenor, sir.

I can make you the greatest, most famous tenor in the world. I know you're too young to understand, but I'm afraid my time has run out. My son, I was waiting to pass this gift onto you until you were old enough to choose it, but...I do hope you don't hate me for it. There will be a price, but I think you'll find it worthwhile.

The boy Libretto remembers the bite, the strength he felt as his father gripped him, the way he cried and resisted but couldn't break free. He'd never known his father to be anything but gentle.

It was that same night that the boy Libretto stood watching the church burn, heard the screams, saw the windows broken from the inside and arms, legs, torsos trying to escape.

The fever began in the orphanage, nine months after his father was incinerated in Van. Alone among the other orphans, he first felt the monster stir.

Madrid Times, April 24, 19______
CARMEN

The Madrid Theater's production of *Carmen,* starring Libretto Santiago and Magdelena Basco, is a colorful cornucopia of Spanish delights. Bizet's opera, which is set in Spain but sung in French, is a feast of Spanish sensuality, and Basco in the title role, smoldering with fire. The Barcelona singer is born to play the flirtatious, boycrazy Carmen.

But the stage stealer is newcomer Libretto Santiago as Don Jose. Armenia-born Libretto Santiago is making his first Spanish appearance in this role, and he brings a depth of character and maturity rarely seen in a young tenor, a quality usually earned after much experience. Santiago seems fated for stardom, and the onstage chemistry between he and Basco is electric. We hope to see much more of Libretto Santiago here in Madrid.

The Forbidden Story: Part Three

Backstage. Closing night, Magdelena Basco in her dressing room, surrounded by flowers and cards. Pasty makeup covers her pale skin, her lion's mane streaked with the Spanish sun, mascara eyes thick as pudding. She removes layers of pancake makeup, ruddy cheeks exposed when Libretto knocks softly and enters. His own makeup is smudged with the shine and sweat of stage lights. His dark hair is slicked and darkened with shoe polish, his eyebrows drawn heavily.

Magdelena is expecting him. This is to be their goodbye.

"Come with me," he says again. "Come with me and we can be the greatest duet the world has ever heard."

"But..."

"Come, they're waiting for us! You'll have to trust me, though. My ways are a bit unconventional and maybe even a bit frightening."

"I could never be frightened of you."

"I have a lot of secrets. They're not pretty."

"I have no use for pretty things, my love."

The New York Times, February 22, 19___

MADAME BUTTERFLY

For those of you who saw the premiere of *Madame Butterfly* over the weekend you may still be recovering. Puccini's magnificent opera has never been performed with the same on-stage chemistry as that between Spain's sweetheart, Magdelena Basco, now Magdelena Santiago, and her real life husband, Libretto Santiago. Marriage alone could not have produced such a fire between these two newlyweds. As the young geisha, Cio Cio San, and the officer of the U.S. Navy, B.F. Pinkerton, the Santiagos' famed duet at the end of Act One has never been performed as convincingly. Cio Cio's naïve conviction, and resulting despair, grips one with the kind of universal necessity operas are written for.

URSULA

How does the story end?

LIBRETTO

There is no ending, it continues.

URSULA

But there must be an ending. All stories have endings.

LIBRETTO

No. Besides it doesn't matter.

URSULA

Of course it matters! A story without an ending is not worth writing.

LIBRETTO

You promised not to write it.

URSULA

Yes, of course.

But I can't stop writing it. The story is growing stronger; in my belly it is swelling, transforming, the poison is breaking down inside. I am so hot, the blood is boiling in me. The monster lives in me, wants to escape, wants to take over my body and mind. Each time I slip into sleep I dream nightmares of fire and lava, of boiling alive. When I awake I fear that I will find myself changed into one of them, but...oh, this heat. I would do anything to quench this heat!

I am beginning to get a sense of other monsters walking the earth. We look away when we pass each other on the street. We know instinctively, somehow. And they know, too.

~Enter Libretto and Magdelena~

LIBRETTO

If she succeeds you know what it could mean. All our years here completely erased.

MAGDELENA

Who cares about that little girl? Just let her go.

LIBRETTO

She can't leave with our story. She doesn't know how dangerous it could be, even for her.

MAGDELENA

Libretto, you stupid fool. You gave it to her. It's hers.

LIBRETTO

But she was supposed to become like us!

MAGDELENA

Just let her go.

LIBRETTO

She can't leave with our story!

MAGDELENA

What are you going to tell her when she starts asking questions? Are we just going to

chain her here like we've done to ourselves? Do you really think we'll just keep doing this, generation after generation?

LIBRETTO

He's going to find us if she doesn't stop writing it! After all these years!

MAGDELENA

I'm going to be dead soon and then you can do whatever you like.

~pause~

I'm glad she has the story. I wanted her to steal it. She's pretty, isn't she? Just your type, I thought...when I invited her in.

LIBRETTO

Oh, how it feels to be hated by those who once loved you! Better to be widowed, my dear. Better to pretend that love goes on in eternity. Magdelena, my love, remember the way we used to command the stages of Europe? Oh, to lose your love is just too much. I shall kill myself right now! I shall take this knife and plunge it into my heart. Better to die than to live hated like this!

MAGDELENA

No, Libretto. It is I who should kill myself. It is I who has been living half dead all these years. It is I who should take this dagger and slit my throat so that I can no longer hear my own agony! We are the ones who cannot let go, my love. I raise this dagger with welcomed relish!

LIBRETTO

No! You bring shame to my heart. With this vial of poison it is *I* who shall give myself the sweet relief of this world, something I should have done so long ago. Better for me to die and be buried underneath the ground—let this earth be a mausoleum to my worthless life.

MAGDELENA

No, Libretto! It is only honorable that I should smash this candelabra into my skull and die a proper death at the hands of love! Let death burn away my pain!

~enter the maid~

THE MAID

Oh the singing! The singing! I'm so tired of the singing! With the rope it is I who shall end this misery! It is I who shall leave this endless opera! Oh, Virgin de Guadalupe, take pity on me and let heaven be a quiet place!

URSULA (writing)
My Dearest Hugo,

How happy I was to get your letter, how far away you feel from me, now. My darling, tragedy has struck here, tragedy so overwhelming I dare not write it down. I have gotten what I came for, but it has come at a price. My doors are locked at night now, my windows sealed. I have an escort wherever I go, to the market, to the garden, even on the rooftop patio the monsters watch me. Oh Hugo, how infantile of me to go looking for a story so far away from you, as if there were no other way to awaken our muse. How ashamed I am of what I have put you through, and what I may still be putting us both through.

The only time the gate is unlocked is for the mailman. Send me another letter, quickly! Your sweet words might actually save me from this place. Oh Hugo, my darling, I come to you on my knees, begging your forgiveness, the depths of which I cannot tell you here, but hope with all my heart that your love waits for me intact and that I may again lay my eyes on you.

Your most humble and shameful wife,
Ursula

The Forbidden Story: Part Four
The Traitor

In Madrid there was another. He knew of the bargain between Libretto and Magdelena. He cornered Libretto, demanded they meet alone:

THE TRAITOR

You showed up.

LIBRETTO

You thought I wouldn't?

THE TRAITOR

I wasn't sure.

LIBRETTO

Are you ready?

THE TRAITOR

Of course.

LIBRETTO

Are you nervous?

THE TRAITOR

Should I be?

LIBRETTO

I don't know...maybe.

THE TRAITOR

I'm not. Shall we do it here?

LIBRETTO

Are you sure?

THE TRAITOR

I'm sure.

LIBRETTO

I'm not sure what will happen.

The Traitor stands, anticipating. Libretto swallows hard, then grabs his arm and bites. The Traitor doesn't struggle, not once does he even twitch though Libretto bites as hard as he can. When it's over they're both panting and flushed. Libretto wipes saliva from his mouth.

THE TRAITOR

How long does it take?

LIBRETTO

I don't know.

THE TRAITOR

I thought it would happen right away.

LIBRETTO

I don't know anything, I told you that.

THE TRAITOR

Maybe you didn't do it right.

LIBRETTO

Do you feel the heat?

THE TRAITOR

No. I just feel sick.

LIBRETTO

Just wait.

THE TRAITOR

I think you tricked me.

LIBRETTO

I told you I didn't know what would happen.

THE TRAITOR

You're a liar, Libretto!

LIBRETTO

I never promised you anything.

THE TRAITOR

Liar!

~Libretto enters room and rips the paper away from Ursula~

LIBRETTO

I said you could never write about it!

URSULA

But I'm a writer!

LIBRETTO

But you made a bargain.

URSULA

You knew I was a writer when you gave it to me.

LIBRETTO

You'll die before I'll allow it.

URSULA

Then kill me because I cannot stop it...

LIBRETTO

You stupid girl! He'll be coming for us! All these years and now we're revealed—you've given us away! You have to stop writing it.

URSULA

It's growing on its own now.

LIBRETTO

Give it back.

URSULA

It's mine, now. Besides, I've improved it. It will be the great novel of our time.

LIBRETTO

Novel! It's to be an opera!

URSULA

Novel!

LIBRETTO

Opera! You'll die before I'll allow you to deform my story.

URSULA

Then kill me because I can't stop it!

LIBRETTO

You'll have to kill yourself.

URSULA

What?

LIBRETTO

Quiet! He will be here, soon. Have you begun to write about him?

URSULA

I've just started.

LIBRETTO

Then we should expect him any time.

~A knock on the door~

It's too late.

End of Act One

ACT TWO

Madrid Times, November 13, 20_______

What happened to the Santiagos? Twenty years and not a trace.

Libretto and Magdelena Santiago, once the darlings of the opera, have not been seen on stage in more than two decades, ever since the unexplainable cancelling of their contracts from Prague to Vienna. While speculation has run the gamut, from secret operations to plastic surgeries and even a few alien theories, all we know is the Santiagos disappeared from the public eye abruptly after their final performance of Tosca, played here 20 years ago this weekend. In tribute, here is the original review of Tosca as it appeared in this paper 20 years ago.

TOSCA

Most refreshing in this production of Tosca is the rare pleasure of seeing Libretto Santiago sing the baritone role of Baron Scarpia rather than his usual tenor, a feat rarely achieved even by the most seasoned performer. As Tosca's obsessor and the chief of police, Libretto brings frightening control to the role, and we feel the real fear in Floria Tosca, played by his real life wife, Magdelena Santiago, under his captivity. Used to seeing the Santiagos play starcrossed lovers, it's refreshing to see the fire ignited as the captured Tosca schemes to free herself from the clutches of her captor. If audiences have been inspired by the Santiagos onstage romantic chemistry all these years, they'll be delighted to know that the chemistry is just as strong—if not stronger, when the two are at odds. You root for Tosca all the way up until the moment when she buries the knife in his back, and then gasp with her in anticipation of the repercussions—what have I done?

The Traitor runs, jumps hills, follows the script, rushing from aria to aria towards the climax. Finally! It must be the same Libretto! The same family!

He descends upon Mexico City, following the acts of the opera. The Itza and The Popo create large black volcanic gulfs in an otherwise endless twinkle of lights, the Torre Latinamericanos a solitary lighthouse. The neon grows larger as he descends, veins of color crisscrossing the sprawl, through the tight, cobbled streets of the Zocalo and across the Palace de Presidentes, through the Ciudadella marketplace fringed with guitars from Michoacan and black clay from Oaxaca and silver from Taxco and posters of Frieda and Diego and Zapata, down the long stretch of Avenida Reforma where poor Mexicans sell bobby pins during red lights, then, sailing along the canals of Xochimilco in boats painted worn shades of pink, green, yellow, red, baby blue, and finally cresting the hills to look upon the once empty bowl of Mexico City now filled with a blanket of smog and 20,000,000 people.

He's following the music. He hasn't considered what might happen when he meets the girl. He sniffs at the bus station, picks out her way of travel...

The bus driver suddenly crosses himself:
head, heart, shoulder, shoulder, lips,
which starts a chain reaction through
the bus
head, heart, shoulder
head, heart
head, heart, shoulder
heart, shoulder
heart, shoulder, shoulder
shoulder shoulder
shoulder lips
shoulder shoulder lips

Lips lips
lips

lips

heart, shoulder, shoulder

lips

kiss rosary beads.

kiss rosary beads.

The maid showed him into the kitchen.

URSULA

Hugo! You found me!

HUGO

~looking at her belly~

I see you've found something, too. Is it the rest of the story?

URSULA

Oh Hugo, it's the most amazing story. But I've been forbidden to write it. Oh Hugo--

HUGO

Do you still love me?

URSULA

What? Of course, more than anything.

HUGO

Then you must help me destroy them.

URSULA

What?

HUGO

Poor girl, how was I to know what kind of story you would find? How were you to know you'd find exactly what you shouldn't?

URSULA

What are you talking about?

HUGO

Check page 41. You wrote it.

URSULA

The Traitor?

HUGO

Yes, my dear. And you know what you are now, don't you?

URSULA

I'm a monster. I regret it.

HUGO

Once you turn you are indeed one of them. But right now you are one of us. Join me in destroying them.

URSULA

But I don't want to destroy them.

HUGO

Don't sentimentalize these people—they care nothing for you! They will betray you and then make it seem like you betrayed them. You're already sick—I can see the sad sickness in you. The moment you turn you are at his mercy again—in fact, I'll have to kill you myself. But help me kill him first and we'll both be free. He calls me The Traitor but he is the one who lies.

~pause~

Have you been having fun, in the bed of another, my dear? You owe me this.

~they're circling, eyes locked~

Write me to him, it's time.

~pause~

Write! Don't just stand there—write! Write our confrontation. You should start with me alone on the stage. The lighting should be dramatic, oranges and reds and purples, and a spotlight on...

~Hugo stands alone in the middle of the stage. The lighting is dramatic, oranges and reds and purples~

HUGO

(Aria)

Half Alive, Half Dead

~Enter Libretto~

LIBRETTO

Should I say 'we meet again' or would that be too cliché even for an opera?

HUGO

You're the one who's been hiding, Libretto.

LIBRETTO

Oh Hugo, why do we have to hate each other? I did what you asked of me.

HUGO

I need the story.

LIBRETTO

It cannot be done.

HUGO

Oh, but it can! Why do you think I sent the girl?

LIBRETTO

You mean the thief.

HUGO

What is hers is mine. She is my wife.

~Enter Ursula, huge with pregnancy~

LIBRETTO

I should have known! She's stolen my story and turned it into a common novel! It was to be the greatest opera ever written!

URSULA

You just hate me because I cared about the story more than you did. You hate thinking that I deserve to have it more than you do.

~enter Magdelena~

MAGDELENA

We all wanted this story. You should have it, you both deserve each other.

HUGO

Magdelena, you haven't aged a bit, I see.

MAGDELENA

Nor you. You're as ghastly as ever.

HUGO

You were always between us. Always Magdelena, Magdelena. I am so tired of that name!

LIBRETTO

Don't blame Magdelena. She shouldn't pay for the sins of my father.

MAGDELENA

Oh, but I pay! And pay! The only thing I've ever loved was the stage, and you both took it away from me! Hugo, if you hate me so much, then end my suffering. Let me at least die in front of an audience!

HUGO

I can do better than that. I've composed a requiem. It's a duet.

~hands out sheet music~

MAGDELENA

Yes! A requiem!

LIBRETTO

I'll never sing your requiem!

HUGO

So this is your first note...It begins "Now the ending finally draws near..."

~insert some "rehearsal" language here~

MAGDELENA

Now the ending finally draws near. Now the curtain may finally close! My love, we met on the stage. We fell in love on the stage. Let us die together on the stage!

HUGO

Libretto, this is your part. Sing, "No, my love—"

LIBRETTO

This is absurd! I will not sing it.

MAGDELENA

You coward! You've taken away everything else from me, do not deny me my death scene!

LIBRETTO

No my love, after all these years!

MAGDELENA

The curtain is closing, red velvet against the sky. Again the warm spotlight on our pale skin. Again the silence of the crowd.. Oh, to bathe in this moment forever, one heartbeat, one breath, one death together! Let us melt to the stage floor once more forever!

LIBRETTO

Oh my love, you are dying! I've lost to my enemy—The Traitor has won!

~pause~

I'm not singing this!

MAGDELENA

I hate you!

LIBRETTO

The Traitor has won! Composer, you have killed us with your requiem. We are released from this terrible nightmare. It ends as I always feared.

MAGDELENA

I'm dying! I'm dying! Oh Libretto, I betrayed you, I let her in, I told her we had a story that would change everything, I told her you would give it to her.

LIBRETTO

No, my love, it is I who have betrayed you! I'll never forget you as Carmen.

MAGDELENA

Or you as Romeo. Oh my love, take thee this poison, and I live no more.

~Magdelena dies~

HUGO

You thought I would just slink away like a fool! You underestimate me, Libretto!

LIBRETTO

I did what you asked!

HUGO

You ruined it! Now I'm left with only one gift, Libretto—this. I wrote you a very special dying aria. You might as well sing it before I kill you.

LIBRETTO
(Aria)

O Father!

~Libretto dies~

~enter The Maid~

THE MAID

Too many years I've spent in this house.

Heaven I'm coming for you!

~The Maid dies~

HUGO

Ursula, we're free! The story is ours! Come kiss me beautiful girl!

URSULA

Get away from me! I don't know you.

HUGO

It's me, Hugo Leonard. Your adoring husband.

URSULA

I just watched my adoring husband slaughter two people.

HUGO

Those weren't people. Those were monsters.

URSULA

We are the monsters, darling.

HUGO

Ursula, you must give me the story. You wouldn't know what to do with it anyway!

URSULA

I won't write another word of this cursed thing!

HUGO

That is no longer up to you, my dear.

URSULA

I won't write it.

HUGO

You will!

~grabs her hair~

URSULA

Hugo!

HUGO

You're not really going to keep pretending, are you? You will not leave here until you finish that story!

~cage door slams~

I hate this story. I hate the Muse. I hate everyone involved in this nightmare and I hate myself. Had anyone tried to warn me when I boarded that plane for Mexico City, I never would have believed them. I don't want to write it anymore. But I can hardly keep it at bay. Oh Muse, please go away! The poison is breaking down inside. My poetry is becoming erratic, words spinning upside down and
backwards.   The words won't b

ehave for me, anymore.
Oh Muse! Save me from myself!

The Muse unwinds down the long stairs as the organ bells grow more urgent. The hiss of fog hides her approach, a beacon sweeps through the clouds, calling the maddened masses to the rocks. She sings in a pitch that makes dogs scream, coloratura and ethereal. Figures emerge through the fog offering gifts, icons, half-finished artistic projects beseeching her to intercede—oh Muse, forgive me, please return, I need you. Since you left it has sat just like this, unfinished...

In Spain they call it *duende*, that mysterious darkness that gives life to creative projects. A goblin of good fortune. The shadow of inspired fire.

Trailing the end of the line a young girl with short hair carries a book, hands it to the Muse. It is entitled *The Monster Opera*.

"If you turn away now, you turn away forever."

"I understand."

The Muse slowly opens the book then lowers it so that the audience can see...blank pages as she rifles through the story. Blank pages forever.

The Muse closes the book hard and the story ruptures and gushes from between Ursula's legs. She falls, her white dress soaked in manuscript pages. The poet writhes and expels the story she is not allowed to write—the church in Armenia and the genocide and the orphanage and the misty form of a monster disguised as an angel and the house in Mexico City and the baby grand piano with no varnish and the heap of monsters dead in the spotlight—rotted, bloated chunks of paper that leave a strong odor.

The poet births the stillborn mess and cuts the umbilical cord. The story is gone. Amidst the blood and tissue are whole downy sentences, perfectly formed little arias, codas, preludes and finales pooling there, on the floor.

THE END

MUSE

(Aria)

Liber Scriptus

Coda

I Found My Muse Hitchhiking Along Route 85

"What are you doing?" I yell out the window. She's carrying her old black duffel bag with the duct-taped corner and chewed strap.

"Leave me alone," she says, scoping the oncoming traffic.

"Where are you going?"

"Away." She sticks her thumb out but there aren't many cars this time of night.

"Come home. Let's talk about it."

"No."

"What about the manuscript?"

"Screw the manuscript," she says. "Finish it yourself."

Then she darts in front of my headlights and becomes a large reddish fox with black paws, who stares at me for a moment before disappearing into a sewer drain.

ACKNOWLEDGEMENTS

I couldn't have written this without the support of my community, especially Rob Geisen, Jonathan Montgomery, Kona Morris, Leah Rogin-Roper, Nate Jordon, Katharyn Grant, Bryan Jansing, E.B. Giles, Benjamin Dancer, Laura Keenan, Selah Saterstrom, Brian Dickson, Jamey Trotter, David Wagner, Meg Tuite, Nick Morris, Serena Chopra, Patricia Morrison, Alicia Fisher, Dan Donan, my children Van Yoho and Felix Kachadourian, and Eron Johnson, whose antique warehouse inspired much of this story.

Special thanks to Erik Wilkins, Marta Burton, Sue Ryplewski and Scott Ryplewski, who lent their voices and talents to make *The Monster Opera* come alive on stage.

And most importantly to my creative partner, composer Nick Busheff, who has nurtured and supported so many of my ideas and didn't tell me I was crazy when I suggested writing an opera.

ABOUT THE AUTHOR

Nancy Stohlman's first novel, *Searching for Suzi: a flash novel (Monkey Puzzle Press, 2009),* started the flash novel genre; she's also the editor of numerous books including *Live From Palestine (South End Press, 2003)* and *Fast Forward: The Mix Tape (Fast Forward Press, 2010)*, an anthology of flash fiction that was a finalist for a Colorado Book Award. A sought after performer, musician, and lecturer, she currently resides in Denver, where she spends her days as a writing professor and her nights as the lead singer of the lounge metal band Kinky Mink. Find out more about her at www.nancystohlman.com

Photo Credit: Lynn Hough/And Everything Else Photography

ABOUT THE COMPOSER

Nick Busheff is an award-winning musician, composer and director living in Denver, Colorado. For more information go to: nickbusheff.com or nickbusheff.wordpress.com